Winter of the Black Weasel

a tale based on a Newfoundland Micmac Legend

Tom Dawe
illustrated by Anne MacLeod

Breakwater Books
P.O. Box 2188
St. John's, Newfoundland A1C 6E6

Canadian Cataloguing in Publication Data

Dawe, Tom

Winter of the black weasel

ISBN 0-920911-16-1

I. MacLeod, Anne. II. Title.

PS8557.A93W56 1988 jC813'.54 C88-098607-7
PZ7.D38Wi 1988

The Publisher acknowledges the support of the Canada Council which has helped make this publication possible.

The Publisher acknowledges the financial support of the Cultural Affairs Division, Department of Culture, Recreation and Youth, Government of Newfoundland and Labrador, which has helped make this publication possible.

In Memory of John Paul
of Badger's Brook
who told his version
of the legend

and Frank G. Speck
who wrote it down
in Beothuck and Micmac (1922)

Long ago, long before any white people had settled on the big misty island of Newfoundland, the Micmacs and the Red Indians lived there together in peace. It was a free and bountiful time back then.

The two tribes were sheltered in a woodsy cove on the west coast where salmon teemed in the brooks and big moon-eyed cod swarmed in the bay.

It was a time too when lofty birch whispered to the beaver and flocks of fowl on the autumn sky cast fertile shadows across the berry grounds.

The two tribes shared much together in their cove, especially one large splendid canoe which took them miles across the bay in search of the seal, the bird, and the berry places. But each year, with the first fall of snow, the canoe was beached near the village to await spring.

Through many long winters, the canoe waited, like some giant cradle upturned in the snow. During these cold, stormy spells, the land was dominated by frost demons and the north wind.

One late afternoon in mid-winter, as frost cracked in the twigs, a group of young Micmacs and Red Indians were playing together near the beached canoe. They were having too much fun to notice a solitary animal staring down at them from a hill above the cove.

A shiny black weasel, low on the crusty snow, had crept cautiously to the edge of the woods. It hunched beneath the dark boughs, watching, tilting its head, never taking its eyes off the young people below.

The creature remained there watching for some time before it left its perch. Then, stretching its long body, it slithered down the slope towards the village.

A Micmac boy was the first to spot the weasel. Quick as a trout in fly-time, the young fellow grabbed a club and chased the creature. But the weasel moved like the wind, snaking its way into a deep tunnel under the big canoe.

Soon most of the other boys had joined in the hunt. They whooped and chuckled in a chain around the canoe, poking their wooden spears into the burrow. But the crafty animal would not come out.

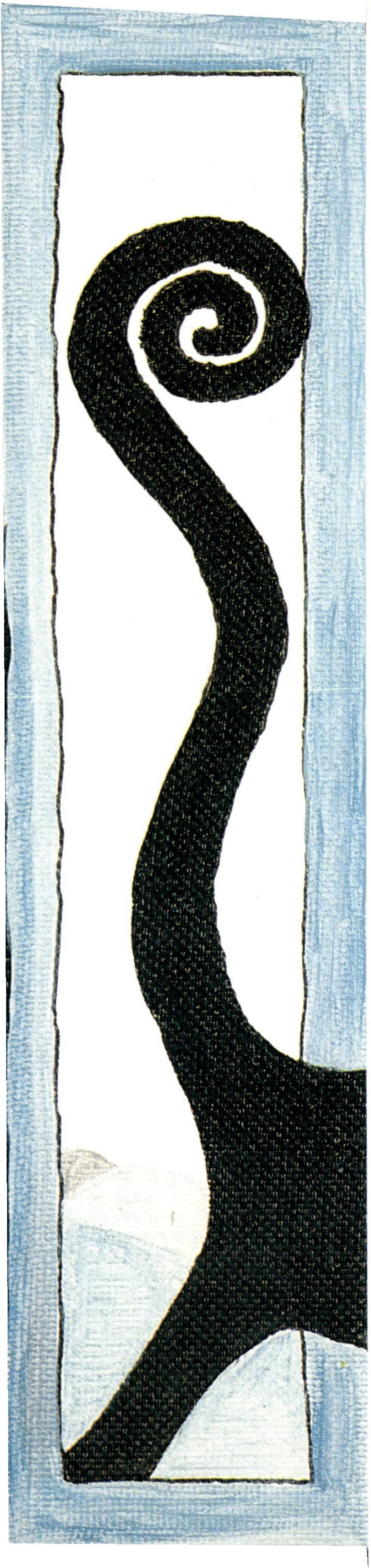

Suddenly, one of the Red Indian boys – he who had not joined in the hunt– ran towards the group. He seemed to be out of breath. He waved his arms wildly.

"Stop," he screamed. His eyes were wide and shining. His long hair lifted on the wind. "Stop, you don't know what you are doing."

But the others just laughed at the young Red Indian and tried to ignore him. They kept probing their spears into the tunnel, trying to flush the weasel out.

Now the Red Indian got angry. "Stop! Stop before it's too late!" he shouted. "It's an evil sign! The weasel is never black in the winter!"

The young hunters just sneered at him. They started to push the Red Indian away from them.

"You're weak...and foolish," one of them yelled.

"Go home," they taunted, waving their spears at him.

As the argument raged, the weasel watched from the shadows, its beady eyes glistening; its sleek body as still as the icicle hanging from the gunnel of the canoe.

The creature was still watching as the frustrated hunters turned homeward, taunting the young Red Indian as they went.

That night, huddled by the fire, with long shadows flickering on the wall, the Micmac boy who had chased the weasel moved closer to his father and told him about the animal under the canoe.

As he listened, his father grew troubled. "Leave that beast alone," he warned, shaking his finger and drawing the blanket closer around them.

The boy was silent. Staring up into his father's eyes, he felt like a small child again.

Outside, in the dark, the wind went by, hissing across the snow.

"No weasel is black in the winter," his father continued. "Stay away from it.... Something evil has come among us, my son."

In the bitter, uneasy days that followed, the Micmac boy could not shake the weasel from his mind. A strange mood crept over him. He was silent most of the time. He did not want to be with his friends anymore. Like a solitary raven, he perched near the edge of the woods, watching the other young people at play.

One late afternoon the Micmac boy found himself alone in the shadow of the big canoe. There, in the frosty stillness, he thought he could hear the weasel whispering. In his mind he could hear too the warnings of his father and his former friend, the young Red Indian, telling him to turn and run away.

But the Micmac boy was helpless now. The tunnel beckoned him. He stood there staring into a darkness deeper than the falling night.

Suddenly the beast emerged. It stood there, strangely stiff, sharp against the snow.

The boy attacked it with a club. He struck again and again, a mad flurry of blows.

The creature lay dead and bleeding in the twilight.

Shivering like an aspen leaf, the boy flung the club away. He fled from the spot as fast as his legs could carry him.

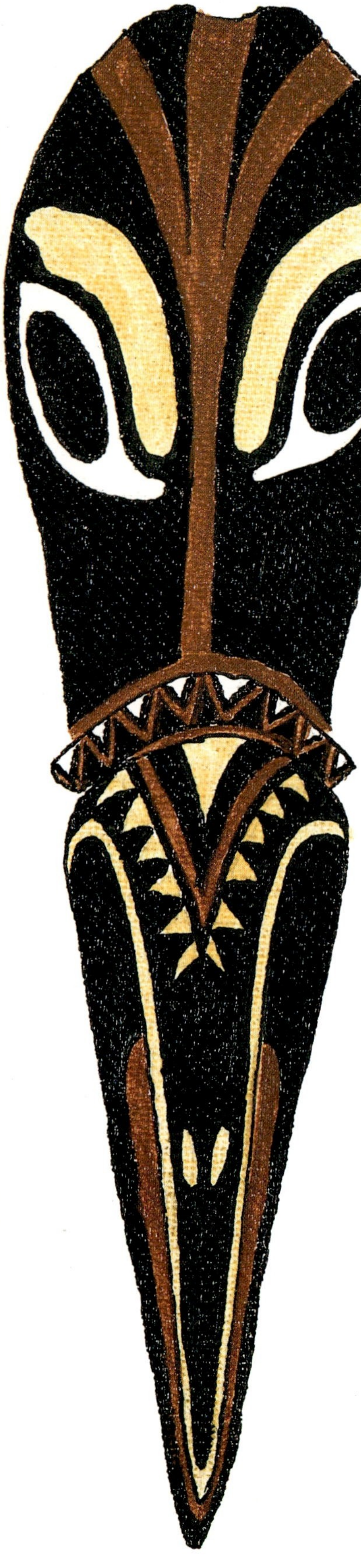

Next morning the Red Indian boy was the first to discover the weasel carcass splayed on the snow. He who had warned them about the beast was now enraged. He wanted to strike out at them, especially when he remembered the way they had laughed in his face and jeered at him. In his anger, he grabbed a club and went looking for the others.

Soon the young Red Indian was wrestling with the Micmac boy who had killed the weasel. It was a terrible quarrel. Jays screamed high in the rampikes above them. Big ravens mocked from the spruce tops.

The other young people joined the fight.

A dark shadow was spreading across the cove and the elders could do nothing to stop it. Soon the whole village was caught up in the battle.

As the day ended, the Red Indian boy lay dead in the lee of the great canoe. His people cried out for revenge. Merciless war gripped the land.

The Red Indians lost ground rapidly. Eventually they were defeated No longer able to live on the coast in peace with the Micmacs, they were forced to flee to the wild interior. A sad, wary people, few in number now, the Red Indians retreated up a frozen river valley.

With the passing years, old, scattered friends from both tribes would meet sometimes, secretly, and recall those green days before the weasel's curse. But such friends were as dry leaves on the wind.

Years later, in the coldest winter of all, a white man appeared one day to the Micmacs on the coast. A gaunt figure hunched in his dark furs, he came down cautiously from the hill, clutching a long gun in his bony fingers. His smile shone in the frosty air when he offered friendship and trinkets to everybody.

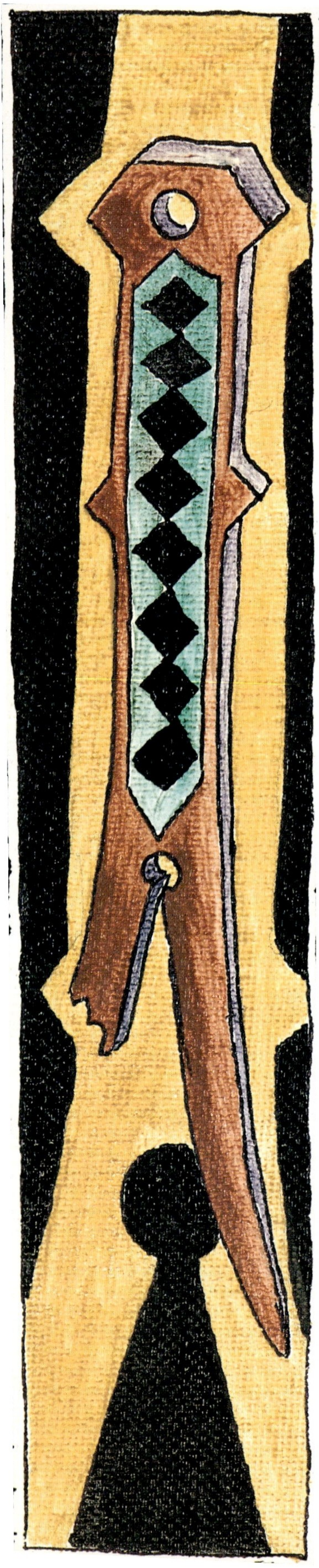

Soon the white man had snaked his way into the heart of the Micmac community. Raiding parties set out for the interior. Now there was winter thunder in the land.

The Red Indians had no way to escape. Isolated, living in mortal fear of all intruders, they could not survive. Never again would they return to the cove of the great canoe, the moon-eyed cod and the salmon streams.

Under the shadow of the black weasel, the small band of Red Indians was doomed. Then one day, like figures sketched on a fog, they disappeared forever from the big misty island of Newfoundland.